GUS and GRANDPA
Ride the Train

Claudia Mills ★ Pictures by Catherine Stock

Farrar, Straus and Giroux
New York

For Christopher Kent Wahl
—C. M.

For Adam and Tarquin
—C. S.

Text copyright © 1998 by Claudia Mills
Illustrations copyright © 1998 by Catherine Stock
All rights reserved
Distributed in Canada by Douglas & McIntyre Ltd.
Color separations by Berryville Graphics / All Systems Color
Printed in the United States of America
Designed by Filomena Tuosto
First edition, 1998

Library of Congress Cataloging-in-Publication Data
Mills, Claudia.
    Gus and Grandpa ride the train / Claudia Mills ; pictures by Catherine
Stock. — 1st ed.
        p.   cm.
    Summary: Gus waves at the train near his grandfather's house, sets up
a toy train, and eventually gets to ride on the train with his grandfather.
    ISBN 0-374-32826-9
    [1. Railroads—Trains—Fiction. 2. Grandfathers—Fiction.] I. Stock,
Catherine, ill. II. Title.
PZ7.M63963Guf   1997
[E]—dc21   97-4988

Contents

"It's the Train!"

Toot! Toot!
The train whistle
was so far away
that Grandpa
could not hear it.
But Gus did.
"Grandpa!" Gus shouted.
"It's the train!"

"Yippee!" Grandpa shouted back.

When Gus came
to visit Grandpa,
he loved to wave
at the train
that rumbled by
across the street
from Grandpa's house.
Gus felt that it was his job
to wave at the train.
He felt that his waving
helped the train to go faster.
He felt that the train
needed him to wave.
"The train is coming!"
Gus hollered again.

Gus ran outside
as fast as he could.
He opened Grandpa's gate.
He ran down Grandpa's driveway.
He did not want to miss
a single car.

Gus stood by the side
of the road.
He waved at the locomotive.
He waved at a boxcar
and a hopper car
and a tanker car
and a flatcar.

Then Gus saw
Grandpa's dog, Skipper,
outside the gate.
Grandpa never let Skipper
run outside the gate.
Someone must have forgotten
to close the gate—
someone in a big hurry
to wave at a train.
Gus's heart turned
a flip-flop.

"Come here, Skipper!"
Gus shouted.
Skipper ran to the house
next door.

"Grandpa!" Gus yelled.

"Come get Skipper!"

But the train cars
clanked and clattered.
Grandpa could not hear.
Gus did not want to stop
waving at the train.
But he had to go inside
right away to tell Grandpa
about Skipper.
Gus ran fast.

Grandpa hurried outside.

"Skipper!" Grandpa called.

This time Skipper came running.

Gus did not feel like
waving anymore.
He had missed waving
at too many cars already.

Then Gus saw
the last car of the train.
It was a red caboose!
Gus had seen cabooses
in books.
He had never seen
a caboose
on Grandpa's train.
He waved and waved
and waved and waved.

A train man stood
on the back
of the caboose.
The man waved at
Gus and Grandpa and Skipper.
He made the train whistle
blow just for
Gus and Grandpa and Skipper.
Toot! Toot!

Where Is Skipper?

When Gus's daddy
was a little boy,
he lived at
Grandpa's house.
Grandpa was
his daddy.
One day Grandpa
said to Gus,
"I think your daddy's
old toy train
is around here somewhere."

Gus and Grandpa looked
in the closet
under Grandpa's stairs.
A broom handle
fell down on Grandpa.
But there was no train.

They looked
in Grandpa's hall closet.
A pair of galoshes
fell down on Gus.
But there was no train.

19

Then they took Skipper out back,
and they looked
in Grandpa's shed.

Grandpa's shed was so old
that the roof sagged.
It was so old
that the door stuck.
Grandpa's shed was dark
and dusty
and musty,
full of cobwebs
and dead leaves
and bugs.
It made Gus's nose tickle.
It made him sneeze.

Gus's parents did not like
Grandpa's shed.
But Gus wanted to have a shed
just like it someday.
Everything in the world
he could ever want
was in Grandpa's shed.
Gus saw a broken wheelbarrow
and a rusty bicycle
and a cracked dog-food bowl
and Grandpa's plastic Christmas tree
with all the ornaments
still on it.

Grandpa pointed to
the faded red-and-blue box
with Daddy's train.
Gus sneezed three times.
"Hurray!" he shouted.
Gus climbed up
onto a pile of boards.
An old bird's nest
fell down on Skipper.
Gus grabbed the train.
He ran back
to Grandpa's house,
sneezing joyfully all the way.

Grandpa helped Gus
set up the train.
The train had a boxcar
and a hopper car
and a tanker car
and a flatcar,
just like the big train.

Grandpa helped Gus build
a town for the train
from scraps of wood
and flowerpots
and empty rolls
of toilet paper.

When the train was finished,
it was time for supper.
Grandpa filled Skipper's bowl.
Grandpa called Skipper.
Skipper didn't come.
"Gus," Grandpa said,
"did you leave
   the gate open again?"

"No!"

Gus felt like crying.

"I didn't!"

Gus knew that
Grandpa believed him.

"Skipper!"
Grandpa shouted more loudly.

"We'd best go look for him,"
Grandpa said.

"Where is the leash?"

"I left it in the shed,"
Gus said.
Gus walked slowly
back to the shed.
He opened the door.
Out came Skipper!
Skipper had been
in the shed
the whole time.

Skipper ran in circles.
He rolled and barked.
He yelped and yipped.
He sneezed and sneezed
and sneezed and sneezed.

Skipper ran inside
Grandpa's house
and jumped on Grandpa.
He wagged his tail so hard
that he knocked over the train
and the train town, too.
But Gus and Grandpa
were so happy to see him
that they didn't care.

"All Aboard!"

Gus and Grandpa
were going to ride
on a real train!
Mommy and Daddy and Skipper
were taking
Gus and Grandpa
to ride a real
old-time steam engine.

34

First they drove all day
on curvy roads
up and down
cool green mountains.
Gus sang train songs.
Skipper barked along with him.
Gus changed some of the words
for Skipper.
He sang,
"I've been barking
on the railroad."
He sang,
"Riding on that
old barking train."

That night they stayed
in a motel.
Daddy and Mommy were tired
from driving.
Gus was tired from singing.
Skipper was tired from barking.
Grandpa was tired from listening
to the singing and barking.

Early the next day,
Mommy and Daddy and Skipper
drove Gus and Grandpa
to the train station.
"Do you have
the train tickets?"
Daddy asked.

"You bet!"
Grandpa said.
"I have them hidden
in a special safe place."

Mommy and Daddy and Skipper
drove away
to visit some friends.
Gus and Grandpa waited
at the station.
They walked up and down
on the platform.
They looked at the train.

The locomotive
huffed and puffed.
The steam hissed
and whistled.
The air smelled
of smoke and cinders.
Then the conductor called,
"All aboard!"

Gus and Grandpa
climbed onto the train.
Gus felt as if
he were bubbling inside
with happy steam.
"Can I hold my own ticket?"
Gus asked Grandpa.

"Sure," Grandpa said.
  But then Grandpa's face fell.
"I hid the tickets
  in a special safe place,"
  he said.
"But now I cannot remember
  where they are."

Gus felt his happy steam
all blow away.
"Are they in your wallet?"
Gus asked.

Grandpa checked.
"No," he said.

"Are they in your pocket?"
Gus asked.

Grandpa checked.
"No," he said.

"We are not doing well, Gus.
The other day
you forgot the gate.
Then we both forgot Skipper.
Now I have forgotten
where I put the tickets."
Grandpa looked
very, very sad.
"I'm sorry, Gus," he said.

"I know," said Gus.
He felt bad
that Grandpa felt bad.
"It's okay."

Grandpa took off his hat
and scratched his head.
"Wait a minute!
Here they are!
I put them in
my hat band!"
The train whistle blew.

Gus felt his happy steam
bubble over again.
He and Grandpa forgot
a lot of things.
But Gus never forgot
that he loved Grandpa.
And Grandpa never forgot
that he loved Gus.

Slowly the train
chugged out of the station.
Along the tracks,
children shouted and waved
at Gus and Grandpa.
Together, Gus and Grandpa
stood at the window
and waved back.

AD	FF	MU
AV	GR	NC FEB 3 '99
BO	HI	SJ
CL	HO	CN L
DS	LS	

THIS BOOK IS RENEWABLE BY PHONE OR IN PERSON IF THERE IS NO RESER
WAITING OR FINE DUE.   LCP #